For Broomstick Riders and their cats,
and for Claire, Nikki and Eric
R.S.

For Mary O'S,
with much love
M.L.

Bella Donna

Witchling

Ruth Symes

Illustrated by Marion Lindsay

Piccadilly Press • London

First published in Great Britain in 2011
by Piccadilly Press Ltd,
5 Castle Road, London NW1 8PR
www.piccadillypress.co.uk

A catalogue record for this book is available
from the British Library

ISBN: 978 1 84812 165 2

1 3 5 7 9 10 8 6 4 2

Printed and bound by CPI Group (UK) Ltd, Croydon, CR0 4YY
Cover design by Simon Davis
Cover illustration by Marion Lindsay

Chapter 1

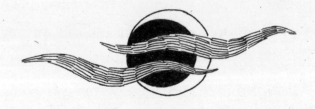

I love Fridays because they're the last day of school before the weekend. And, as I opened my eyes that morning, I remembered I *really* loved this particular Friday, which just happened to be a Friday the thirteenth, because it was my birthday!

All my friends were going to come round after school for my birthday party and I was so looking forward to it. I'd never had a proper party in my own home before. All my other birthdays had been spent at Templeton Children's Home, where I had been left as a baby. Now I was eleven, and this was my first birthday as Lilith's adopted daughter. I had never been happier, and I knew this was going to be the best birthday ever.

Lilith had realised I was a witch as soon as she saw me at the children's home, and she had taken me to live in Coven Road, which is full of witches. It's important that anyone who isn't a witch never sees the true magic of Coven Road and so, every month at midnight, Zorelda — who's the grand sorceress and head of Coven Road — leads all the other witches in casting a spell so that non-witch visitors to Coven Road only see it as a perfectly ordinary road, full of perfectly ordinary people. Because my school friends were coming to my house for my birthday party and were going to be staying for longer than people normally do, the witches had cast an extra strong spell this month.

Everyone at my school knows how much I like anything to do with witches, and love wearing black, but only my friend Sam knows that I really am a witch. Or strictly speaking, a witchling, which is a trainee witch.

It's a bit weird having two lives – an ordinary life going to school and a witch life learning to cast spells – but I wouldn't have it any other way.

The day started perfectly. Lilith had decorated

the breakfast table with balloons at each corner and flowers in the middle and there were lots of presents.

'Happy birthday,' Lilith had said, as soon as I came downstairs with our stripy cat Pegatha – who'd woken me up with a big birthday lick.

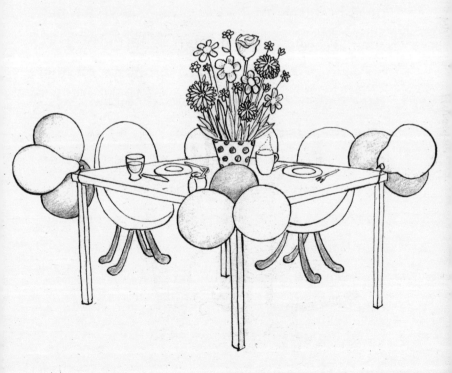

Lilith pulled a stack
of my favourite banana
and blueberry pancakes
from the oven and stuck
a whizzy sparkling
candle in the middle of them.

I felt a bit overwhelmed. This wasn't like my usual birthdays. At Templeton Children's Home we got one present and a birthday tea. Sometimes two people had birthdays on the same day so they had to share the birthday tea. One year I had to share mine with a girl called Stella (she got adopted soon after). When everyone sang 'Happy Birthday', they sang it to both of us at the same time: 'Happy birthday dear Bella-and-Stella . . . Happy birthday to you!' We even had to share the cake and blow out the candles together. It wasn't nearly as much fun as being the only one having a birthday.

'Are those for me?' I whispered to Lilith, my eyes wide at all the presents. Lilith smiled. 'I know there's a lot. I'm afraid I got a bit carried away, but I've never had a daughter to buy presents for before and there were so many things I thought you might like.'

There were parcels with clothes in them and parcels with jewellery – including some beautiful tiny cat-shaped earrings – and parcels with pencils and coloured pens. I loved them all. Lilith obviously understood me so well that she knew what I would like best – and that thought made me even happier.

'I'm saving your very best present for your second birthday party,' Lilith said, smiling.

My second birthday party was going to be a proper witch's birthday party, with all our witch neighbours. I was sure Lilith was saving my special birthday present for then because it was something magical. That had to be the reason! And the magical present I was really *really* hoping that she was going to give me was a witch's book called a grimoire. Lilith writes all

her spells down in her grimoire and every proper witch has one. I wanted to have one too – I'd been wanting one really badly for months. I imagined writing my own spells in the book's creamy-coloured pages with one of my new birthday pens. Even the sound of it felt magical – 'grimm-wharr' . . .

Some grimoires are really old and have been passed down from generation to generation. Lilith's book is over two hundred years old. It was given to her by her mother, who was given it by her mother, who was given it by her mother, and maybe it had even been handed down before then too. Each one of them had added their own spells to it. Zorelda's grimoire – which is on a pedestal in the Ice Palace – is over five hundred years old!

I don't know exactly how old Zorelda is, and Lilith doesn't either, but she's so knowledgeable

I think she might be over five hundred years old too. It's very hard to tell how old some witches are though. I used to think it was because they could magic themselves to be any age they liked as easily as putting on their lipstick, but I've since found out that's not quite the case. Witches' spells aren't usually permanent and they tend to wear off after a while.

I'd already hinted to Lilith that I wanted a grimoire. 'I really love writing,' I told her a couple of weeks ago.

'Maybe you'll be a writer when you grow up,' Lilith said, which wasn't what I meant.

'No, I mean, I *really* love writing spells.'

Lilith still didn't seem to understand, but I think she was just pretending that she didn't. Lilith is very clever and usually we understand each other perfectly. Sometimes we can guess what the other person is going to say even before they've said it. If Lilith was going to give me a grimoire, and I really, really hoped she was, then it would need to be given at a special occasion – and what more special occasion than a witchling's birthday party?

All day long at school I couldn't help thinking about my two birthday parties and wondering what my final present from Lilith was going to be. Everyone said they were really looking forward to coming round, and that just made me look forward to the party even more.

At the end of school I rushed home to get ready. My guests started arriving just before six. I was so excited!

As soon as the doorbell rang, I raced downstairs to open the front door, with Pegatha scampering along behind me. Wherever I am she wants to be too. She's like my very own little cat shadow.

Pegatha was wearing a purple bow so she was dressed up for the party too. Besides Pegatha we have four other cats called Brimalkin, Amelka, Mystica and Bazeeta. I hadn't put birthday bows on them because I didn't think they'd be happy wearing them. They're all Siamese cats and a bit aloof. Mainly they like to sit on the bookshelves and watch what's going on and look down their noses at Pegatha. Pegatha doesn't care what they think of her, though, because she's too busy having fun.

I had a feeling that Sam would be the first to arrive. He's my oldest friend. We've known each other since we were babies and both lived at Templeton Children's Home.

As I said before, Sam is my only friend from school who knows the truth about Coven Road or that I'm a witchling. And I'm one of the few people who don't mind that he can't resist picking up frogs or getting a closer look at bugs and animals he finds. That's just Sam for you.

I pulled the front door open and there he stood, dressed smartly for the party and holding a large box wrapped in bright wrapping paper. 'This is for you.'

'Thanks,' I said, smiling, and let him come inside.

'Hello, Sam,' said Lilith as she put some cupcakes out on the table.

'Hello, Lilith.' Sam grinned.

Sam and Lilith get on really well, which is lucky because the last time the two of them met, Sam had been turned into a toad and Lilith had to change him back into himself. Afterwards Sam said he didn't mind being a toad for a little while because he loved wildlife and had always wondered what it would be like to be a toad and now he knew. But even he wouldn't want to be stuck as one forever.

'Can I open it?' I asked Lilith. At Templeton

Children's Home we'd always had to wait until after the cake was cut to open our present.

Lilith smiled. 'Of course you can — it's your birthday.'

'Come on!' Sam said. 'I've spent ages growing it for you.'

Growing it for me? I ripped off the wrapping paper and opened the box to find a bushy purple plant.

'It's called a buddleia,' Sam said. 'Butterflies really like them. I grew it myself from a cutting.'

'That's really clever of you, Sam. Thanks,' I told him.

'It's beautiful,' said Lilith, 'and you're right, Sam, butterflies do love them.'

Sam's mad about all kinds of wildlife, even frogs and toads, which is just as well because he now lives with Trevor and Tracey, who run the local Woodland Wildlife Centre. Trevor and Tracey adopted Sam a little while after Lilith adopted me. They're the perfect parents for him, just like Lilith is the perfect mum for me.

When we were at Templeton Children's Home, Sam and I always called the families we hoped would eventually adopt us our

Forever Families and I was
very happy that we had both
found a Forever Family.
Sam was smiling at me like
he knew what I was thinking.

He was the only one of my friends who really
understood quite how special it was to have a
birthday party with your own friends and your
own family in your own home.

Pegatha purred and wound herself around
Sam's legs.

'Hello, Pegatha,' Sam said, giving her a stroke.
'You look very pretty in your purple bow.'

Pegatha rubbed her head against him and he
stroked behind her ears – Pegatha loves being
stroked there. The other cats looked a bit jealous.

We played with Pegatha until the other guests
arrived, but I couldn't wait for the party to begin!

Chapter 2

Ellen's mum dropped off Angela, Ellen and Rajni a few minutes later. I think Pegatha thought they'd come to visit her, and it was true they were all keen to see her because I was always talking at school about Pegatha and the things she gets up to. Ellen and Rajni hadn't met Pegatha before but Angela had.

'This is for you, Pegatha,' Angela said, dangling a little toy mouse in front of her.

Pegatha batted the mouse with her paw and Ellen and Rajni laughed.

'She's so cute!' said Ellen.

Pegatha looked at Ellen and Rajni and then she batted at the toy mouse again to make them laugh some more. Pegatha's so funny sometimes.

'And this is for you, Bella,' Rajni said. She handed me a small present wrapped in shiny gold paper with an orange plastic flower stuck to it. 'But be careful because it's quite fragile.'

Inside the wrapping paper was bubble-wrap and inside the bubble-wrap was a diamond-shaped glass prism.

'You put it in your window,' Rajni said, 'and when the sun shines through it, it will make rainbows dance around your room.'

'Wow! That's amazing. Thank you.' I couldn't wait to see how it looked so everyone, including Pegatha, followed me up to my room. I stood on a chair and tied the string of the prism round my curtain rail in front of the window. The sun was shining and a sunbeam caught the prism, and

rainbows were suddenly everywhere in my room. It was like magic!

I love my room. At Templeton Children's Home I had to share a room with a few other girls, but now I live with Lilith I have a room of

my own – although Pegatha is in it just as much
as me and I'm sure she thinks that my bed is
really her bed because it's one of her favourite
places for sleeping. I've got a poster of a unicorn
on one wall and a picture of the stars from the

TV show *Dark Dreamer* on another. Lilith said I could paint the walls any colour I like. There is a spell for changing furniture and wall colourings – there's a spell for just about everything. Lilith taught me the colour-changing spell and sometimes I chant the spell and change my room in an instant just for the fun of it. It doesn't last, of course, because the spell wears off. I don't mind though, because I like the walls the colour that Lilith and I painted them best, which is a soft lavender – one of the colours of magic.

'You're so lucky having your own room,' Ellen said, enviously. 'I have to share with my little sister and she's always leaving her clothes and toys all over the floor and then Mum tells me to pick them up. It's so not fair.'

Pegatha twirled around Ellen's legs as if she were trying to console her.

'And we can't even have a cat because my dad's allergic to them,' she continued, as she stroked Pegatha.

I watched the prism dangle down next to my precious witch mobile – that had been with me when I was left on the steps of Templeton Children's Home eleven years ago – and we watched the rainbows twirl around for a few minutes. Then the sun disappeared behind some clouds, and the rainbows faded away. It was a shame to see them go.

Angela handed me her present. She had bought me a make-up bag. 'Nice colour, don't you think?' she said. 'For a change.'

The make-up bag was bright pink. Angela is crazy about the colour pink. If she was the prime minister she'd make everyone in the country wear it, I think!

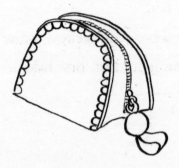

Angela knows I like black, black and more black. It's a joke between us that she always wears pink and I always wear black.

'Thanks,' I said. I liked it because it would remind me of Angela.

'Happy birthday,' Ellen said, and she handed me a soft, squishy parcel. The wrapping paper had a little cat blowing out the candles of a birthday cake on it.

'Thank you,' I said, and started to unwrap the present.

'You told me so much about Pegatha that as soon as I saw it, I thought of you – I hope you like it,' Ellen said.

Inside was a beautiful yellow straw bag with a blue cat embroidered on one side.

'It's lovely,' I said.

Pegatha tried to climb into the bag.

'No, Pegatha – it's not a cat house!' I said, picking her up as everyone laughed. I'd have to make sure I kept the straw bag somewhere Pegatha couldn't play with it or it would be ruined in no time by her sharp little claws.

'Hello,' called a voice from downstairs.

It was Verity. She's Lilith's niece and so she's now my cousin. She's a few years older than me, and a witchling too.

Verity came up the stairs and into my

bedroom. She looked very sophisticated in a red dress and black boots.

When I'd first invited Verity to my non-witch friends birthday party she hadn't been sure if she would come or not. 'It's just for kids,' she'd said, scornfully. Verity likes to make out that she's very mature. I am a little bit in awe of her because she acts so grown up but then sometimes she'll forget and there doesn't seem to be much of an age difference between us after all.

'Is this where the party's at?' she joked, although of course she knew it was. Most of the time I think I understand and like Verity, but every now and again she'll say or do something that confuses me and makes me wonder if she's really being mean and isn't nice at all.

Ellen and Rajni immediately wanted to know where Verity got her dress and boots from because they wanted to get some just the same. Verity has that effect on people.

'Happy birthday,' she said to me. 'This is for you.'

Her present was inside a small, black drawstring bag.

'Thank you,' I said, peering inside.

Verity had brought me lotions, and some pretty black nail polish with glitter in it.

'I love it!' I said. I could keep it in my pink make-up bag. Ellen and Rajni and Angela loved the nail polish too. Verity painted some on everyone's fingernails, except for Sam's, of course – he'd gone to look at the newts in our pond when the nail polish had come out. When Verity had finished painting our fingernails she painted our toenails too and by then almost all of my birthday nail polish had gone. For a moment I was a little upset that my present had been used

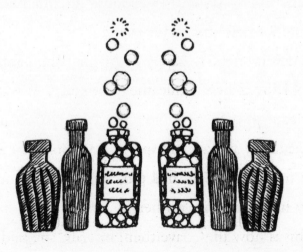

up, but everyone was so happy with their nails that I didn't really mind.

'Even our toes are friends,' Angela said, laughing, as we all wiggled our newly painted toenails together.

Next, Verity helped us curl our hair and crimp and braid it into fun styles – we couldn't stop giggling! By then we were all getting hungry.

I didn't want to have sandwiches at my birthday tea like we had at Templeton Children's Home, so Lilith had made us all individual pizza bases and we put whatever topping we liked on them. Everyone was happy to play all the party games I loved best while they cooked – it was really fun!

I made my pizza extra spicy. It was so spicy it made me sneeze. Sam had pineapple on his and Verity had anchovies on hers.

'This is how they have them in Italy,' she said.

I think Pegatha wanted some of Verity's anchovies. She gave her a hungry stare.

'Stop looking at me like that Pegatha!' said Verity.

Verity and Pegatha don't really get on very well.

When Lilith came out with my birthday cake everyone sang, 'Happy Birthday'.

'Don't forget to make a wish before you blow out the candles,' Verity said to me.

But I was already so happy that I didn't know what to wish for, so I wished that I could save my wish for when I needed it.

After the birthday tea, we watched a funny movie about magical cats. Lilith came in with a bowl of popcorn and Pegatha pounced on a bit that fell on the floor. She tried to eat it but decided she didn't like it and spat it out.

'Cats don't like popcorn,' I told her as she stared at the popcorn piece.

'Try one of these instead,' Lilith said. She'd made all the cats some special birthday fish treats so they had something nice to eat too. Pegatha liked her fish treats much better than popcorn. All the cats particularly liked the ones that had anchovies in them. Bazeeta liked them so much he tried to eat one of Amelka's too. She wasn't very pleased with him and swatted him with her paw.

At nine o'clock, Trevor and Tracey came in their jeep to pick Sam up.

'Thanks for a great birthday party,' Sam said.

'Thanks for growing me a butterfly plant,' I told him.

Rajni's dad took Angela, Ellen and Rajni home. 'You know it's very strange,' he said. 'I pass by this way every day but I've never noticed this street before.'

I tried not to giggle. The monthly protection spell stops anyone who hasn't been invited into Coven Road from being able to see it.

'Hope you have more rainbows in your room tomorrow, Bella,' Rajni said, as she climbed into the car. I hoped so too.

Lilith and I waved them off. 'Thanks for coming. And thanks for all my presents,' I called after them.

It was sad to see them go. I'd had such a good afternoon that I didn't want it to end. I was so pleased that I'd been allowed to invite my friends to our house for my birthday party, even if they couldn't see the real, magical Coven Road. We'd still had a great party — my first ever proper birthday party in fact.

I looked up at Lilith and she smiled at me.

My birthday wasn't over yet. Now I was about to have a second party!

Chapter 3

As soon as my friends left Coven Road, it turned back into its usual magical self, ready for my next birthday party. It was nice to get to stay up so late – Lilith is usually very strict about bedtimes. As the stars and moon came out, all

the houses looked different and exciting in their own ways. Lilith and I live in a thatched cottage with roses that are always changing colour around the door. Verity and her mum have six twirling turrets on their house and a window made from rubies. Zorelda, the grand sorceress, lives in an Ice Palace that never melts. Our next-

door neighbour, Mr Robson, has recently added
a statue of a giant spider on top of his house and
the roof even looks a bit like a spider's web.

When he is being his magical self, Mr
Robson likes wearing a cloak made of real, live,
running-about spiders. Luckily Mr and Mrs
Robson's dog, Waggy, seems to like spiders too –

or at least he's always wagging his tail when they're around. And Waggy never seems to mind when a butterfly flies off Mrs Robson's magical butterfly cloak and lands on him.

There's Redbeard, whose beard is so long it almost reaches his knees. He lives with thirteen cats in a house that looks like a pirate's ship, complete with a skull and crossbones flag. Maybe it actually was a pirate's ship once.

And then there's Kelda who lives with her

snakes and alligators in a house in the trees that I call the Tarzan house.

The communal garden in the centre of Coven Road is always pretty with flowers and trees, but when it's being its magical self, it's a place where you could spot just about anything – from unicorns to miniature elephants, to pink and blue flying penguins. There's even supposed to be a dragon or two there, according to Mr Robson, although I've never seen any myself.

I changed into a long turquoise dress for my magical birthday party and Lilith put on her white witch's outfit. All thirty-nine of the witches who live in Coven Road were invited and everyone had said they would come.

Verity changed into her favourite red ball-gown and black top hat for this birthday party. She'd also put on lots of black eyeliner and mascara to make her eyes looke really big.

'Thanks for coming to the party for my school friends,' I said to her as we went outside. 'They all really liked you.' It was strange that Verity never had any of her friends to visit at Coven Road. Or at least none that I'd met.

'Of course they did,' said Verity.

That's what Verity's like sometimes – super sure of herself and that everyone will like her.

Everyone was out in the communal garden already, chatting and laughing and casting spells. Witches and witchlings love performing magic, and people were taking it in turn to perform their favourite spells. Magic is so much fun that if you can do it, you want other people to see that you can do it!

Verity performed a spell that made thousands of tiny coloured stars come sprinkling out of her fingertips when she pointed.

'*Sazarandi mowlerimo zaldina zesar marar,*' she chanted, over and over, as she pointed this way and that.

It was a great spell. Not hard to do — but very dramatic.

Mrs Robson, from next door, did something even more dramatic — she cast a spell so that the butterflies flew off her cloak and started chasing after the magical stars. When they caught one,

the butterflies flashed silver or gold,
just for a second. Then the butterflies
flew back together into a cloak
falling from Mrs Robson's shoulders.
Meanwhile the stars turned into gold
dubloons and dropped into a treasure
chest that appeared beside Redbeard.
Then Kelda shrank the chest until it was
bite-sized and one of her pythons ate it!
Zorelda made a grand entrance
arriving in a carriage that flew
through the air and was drawn by a
silver dragon called Spike who let me
pat his nose and stroke his back.
'I wish I could have a pet dragon,' I
told Lilith, but Lilith just rolled her
eyes, so I knew it wasn't very likely.
'Maybe for my birthday next year?'
I suggested.

As well as the magical tricks, there were all my usual favourite things at the party – the buffet table that can produce any food you can think of (I like fizzy, blue ice cream best, and had lots of that), the magical daisy chain swings (I still haven't worked out which spell keeps them in the air without being attached to anything but people took it in turns to push me high on them) and of course the unicorns with their foal. I never imagined such things even existed before I came to live in Coven Road but now I loved them all.

'This is the best birthday party ever!' I said to Verity. I never wanted it to end.

But Verity wasn't listening to me – she was looking upwards. Then I realised that all the witches were looking up at the sky and so I looked up too.

Something was flying towards us . . .

'It's the Broomstick Riders!' shouted Verity.

The Coven Road witches cheered. I couldn't believe it. Of course I know witches are often portrayed riding broomsticks, but I'd never seen a witch riding one before, although I've seen lots of witches on magic carpets and I like riding on my bedroom rug. It's not the same as a broomstick, though!

Thirty witches on broomsticks flew in formation and swooshed in between each other and did loop the loops and zoomed up and down, spun and twisted and did all sorts of acrobatics before forming themselves into the shape of letters:

HAPPY

BIRTHDAY

BELLA

'They're amazing,' I gasped.

Lilith squeezed my hand. 'Good, aren't they?' she said.

I could only nod my head. I was speechless.

'Happy birthday to our newest witchling, Bella Donna,' said Zorelda, and everyone clapped and said 'Happy birthday' and 'Hear, hear!'

Redbeard said, 'Many happy returns to the landlubber.'

Kelda's snake opened its mouth very wide and hissed, 'Birthday kisses.'

'Time for your special present,' Lilith said, smiling.

How brilliant that I was finally going to get my own grimoire!

Lilith reached behind a tree and handed me a broomstick with a purple ribbon tied round it.

I was so surprised that it wasn't a grimoire that for a moment I was completely still. My face felt frozen. Then I noticed everyone looking at me and I realised I hadn't said anything. 'Thank you. Thank you so much!' I said, smiling at Lilith.

She gave me a huge smile back.

It was a good present, it just wasn't what I had been

expecting. I thought that flying on it might be fun, though. 'Do you think I might be able to fly like the Broomstick Riders?'

The Broomstick Riders were just black specks in the distant sky now. It would be so wonderful to be able to fly like them one day.

'I'm sure you could, if you practised really hard,' Lilith said.

'And hold on tight!' Verity laughed.

'Have *you* got a broomstick, then?' I asked Verity. She sounded like she knew about flying one.

'Of course I have.'

'Why didn't you tell me before? I'd have loved to have seen it.'

'You'd only have wanted to try flying on it.'

Yes, I would have.

'And witchlings aren't allowed to fly until they're eleven.'

Still, I thought it was a bit mean of her not to have told me.

'And do you have a broomstick, too?' I asked Lilith.

'Yes.' She smiled. 'Although I haven't used it in years. It's old magic and most grown-up witches don't use them much any more. They've rather gone out of fashion.'

But I didn't care about that. 'I'm going to fly mine all the time!' I said.

I was so excited thinking about flying like the Broomstick Riders that I *almost* forgot about how much I'd been hoping for a grimoire.

Then I heard a clock striking midnight and the party came to an end.

'Better put an L-plate on that broomstick,' Verity joked as she waved goodbye. 'They're a lot harder to ride than you'd think.'

But I was sure I'd be able to manage. After all,

I could ride a bike. A broomstick couldn't be that different, could it?

I went to sleep thinking about how wonderful my first two birthday parties had been, and how lucky I was to live in Coven Road with Lilith and be a witchling, and how great it had been to do all my favourite things. I dreamed all night of flying loop the loop on my new broomstick.

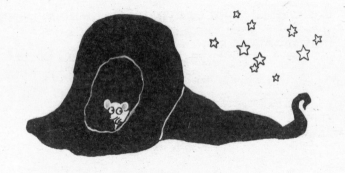

Chapter 4

When I woke up on Saturday, I was a little bit sad. It wasn't my birthday any more and I wouldn't get to do all the fun things I love so much. But then I remembered there was something good about it. Saturdays are my favourite day of the week because I have my spell-casting lesson. All witchlings get to have one spell-casting lesson a week, but I'm extra lucky because my spell-casting teacher is also my mum – Lilith. There are only two witchlings living in Coven Road, me and Verity, so we have our lessons together. She didn't come round until eleven o'clock because we were all very tired from the party the night before.

I wanted to ask Verity about her grimoire. Verity had a broomstick and I hadn't known about that, so the chances were she had a

grimoire as well. I was sure she must have one —
she's lived in Coven Road all her life. No one's
allowed to have spell-casting lessons until they're
ten years old, but as she's older than me, she's
been spell-casting for longer.

It's considered too dangerous for anyone to
cast spells before they're ten. I tried to imagine
what it would be like if baby witchlings were
casting spells all over the place. There would be
giant teddy bears walking down the street and
you'd have to watch out if you were anywhere
near a baby witchling having a temper tantrum!
It'd be chaos, but I thought that it would
probably be very funny too.

'So what's your grimoire like?' I asked Verity,
while Lilith prepared the cauldron for our
lesson.

'My what?' Verity said.

'Your grimoire.'

'I don't have a grimoire,' she said, crossly.

Maybe she was also upset that she didn't have one.

'Why on earth would you think I'd have one? Grimoires are only for fully trained witches – not witchlings like us!'

'What's going on?' Lilith asked, coming out of the kitchen.

'She'd thought I'd got a grimoire,' Verity said.

'Oh no – why would you think that?' Lilith said.

I shrugged. 'I just . . .'

'Verity has lots of fine witch qualities but she isn't ready for her own grimoire yet,' Lilith said.

'But I'll be ready before you.' Verity gave me a black look, which I did my best to ignore.

'I just thought that maybe . . .'

Verity's eyes widened. 'You didn't think you were getting one for your birthday, did you?'

'No,' I lied. But my blushing face gave me away.

'You did!'

'When I was a witchling I can remember desperately wanting a grimoire too,' Lilith said, reassuringly.

So I was only being perfectly normal.

'But you mustn't rush these things. A grimoire is much too dangerous to be given to a witchling,' Lilith went on, and she smiled at me. 'But one day, when you're a full witch, I'm sure you'll have one.'

'Grimoires have to be earned,' Verity said.

'Oh,' I said in a small voice. I hadn't known that. I felt like I'd been working so hard at being a witchling – Lilith was always saying how much potential I had *and* I'd come third in the Witchling Spell Casting Contest even though I was new to magic *and* I'd saved Coven Road from being taken over by the bad witch Rosina Rowan. But it obviously wasn't enough.

'A grimoire in the wrong hands could be very dangerous,' Lilith told us. 'There's so much magic inside most of them that they're almost bursting with it.'

'Is it the grimoires themselves that are magical or the spells written in them?' I asked.

'The spells of course,' said Verity. 'A book can't be magic, can it?'

Lilith frowned. 'I'm not so sure. I think grimoires might have magic of their own too. Would you like to have a look at my grimoire?' Lilith asked us. 'As you both seem so interested in it?'

'Yes!' Verity and I said together.

Lilith went to fetch her grimoire from her bedroom, then held it out to us. 'Here it is.'

The cover was made of leather and there was

an embossed star on the front, just like I'd imagined. It was a bit battered and had old, yellowing pages. It looked like it had been used lots and lots of times.

'How many spells are written in there?' asked Verity, her eyes wide.

'Maybe a thousand or two,' Lilith said with a smile.

'As many as that?' I asked. The book didn't look big enough for thousands of spells to be written in it.

'They must be written in very small writing,' Verity said.

Lilith laughed and shook her head. 'That's one of the many amazing things about grimoires. You can write as many spells as you like in it, put in as many pressed herbs and photographs and thoughts as you want, and it can accommodate them all without seeming to grow any bigger.'

'But how do you find the spell you want when there are so many of them?' I asked.

'The grimoire will show you the one you need,' Lilith said, 'or the spell that you will find most appealing.'

Verity and I squeezed together so that we could both see the spells that appeared and disappeared as we turned the pages. The paper seemed to hum underneath our fingers. I thought it must be very powerful indeed.

'But suppose you were just looking through

the grimoire to see what was in it?' Verity said. 'Not looking for anything in particular – just looking.' As she spoke Verity turned the page and a new spell appeared. It was a love potion spell!

'I didn't mean for that to appear. I don't need a love potion!' Verity said quickly. But she said it with such force that I knew she was lying – there was a boy Verity was interested in!

'So the grimoire isn't just a book – it's a librarian and mind-reader too,' I said in wonder.

Lilith explained that grimoires are such very special, magical books that you have to be very careful when you're around them. They're *so* magical that their spells are particularly powerful, and it would be very easy to cast one by mistake. That's why she needed to be with us when we looked inside her one – in case something happened. But seeing a real one just made me even more desperate than I had been before to have a grimoire of my own.

'Oh look, here's an Agreement Spell,' I said, turning the page.

'Ah yes,' said Lilith. 'It's actually surprisingly easy considering it's a mind spell.'

'What do you mean "a mind spell"?' asked Verity.

'Well,' said Lilith, 'the spells you're learning, as witchlings, are physical spells – you change the way people or things look, or taste, or sound. Mind spells are more dangerous and can change the way people or animals think. They need to be used *very* carefully, so only experienced witches use them. All spells – and especially mind spells – should only be cast after full consideration of the consequences that the spell might have. For instance, you wouldn't really want someone to love you if they didn't do it of their own free will, would you?'

Verity looked a bit embarrassed. 'Of course not – I really don't know why that spell appeared,' she said.

'Most mind spells are very difficult – like that love potion, for instance,' Lilith continued, 'but some, like the Agreement Spell, are a lot easier.'

The pages began turning themselves. Lilith didn't just have spells written in her grimoire. She wrote down her thoughts sometimes, too, including ones about me: *I met Bella today and I know she is supposed to be my daughter . . .* I read.

'Did you really think that?' I asked Lilith.

'Yes.'

'I thought that about you too – that you were supposed to be my mum.'

There were also little squiggly drawings in the grimoire.

'What's that supposed to be?' Verity asked, pointing to a loopy design that looked a bit like a cat.

'Even I'm not sure what that is,' Lilith said, 'but then again, I don't think I drew it. Maybe it was my mother or my grandmother.'

There were also some photographs, old and new, including a school photograph of me. And there were some pressed herbs and flowers with lists of their uses scrawled beside them.

Lilith showed us the first spell she'd written in there, and although I read the faded writing, I didn't say it out loud – just in case. Spells can be very tricky, and sometimes you can end up casting one without even meaning to. That's why we have witchling lessons. Magic can be used for good or bad, and a spell said wrongly – or even said correctly but with the wrong intention behind it – can be disastrous.

'One day, when you're ready, you'll both have your own grimoire,' said Lilith, closing the book. She put it away in her bedroom and then came back downstairs.

'Is it time now?' said Verity, hopefully.

'Yes,' said Lilith.

'Time for what?' I asked.

'We're going to have a different sort of lesson today,' said Lilith.

'Good – I didn't want to have brought it with me for nothing,' said Verity without answering me.

'Time for what? Brought what for nothing?' Why weren't they answering me?

Verity pulled her broomstick out from where she'd hidden it behind the sofa. I would have known it was Verity's broomstick anywhere. Its handle was bright red and instead of just twigs on the end, like my broomstick, her one had bright red roses. Verity's broomstick was beautiful and stylish, just like her, and I couldn't help feeling more than a little envious. Why couldn't I have a broomstick that looked like Verity's instead of one that was so . . . so ordinary?

'Time for your first flying lesson!' said Verity. 'No point having a broomstick and not riding it, is there?' She grinned.

We went out into the back garden.

'Don't you need your broomstick?' I asked Lilith. I wanted her to fly too.

Lilith looked a bit doubtful. 'I haven't flown for so long. Not since I was a witchling.'

'Pleeeeease.'

'All right.'

Lilith ran upstairs again, and came back downstairs with a broomstick that looked as ordinary as mine. I felt a little better about my broomstick.

No one needed a broomstick to travel these days, of course. There were flying carpets for party flying – no one flew around much on them at any other time. Planes were more comfortable than broomsticks to ride on for long flights. Cars and trains could go as fast as broomsticks and were better if it was very cold or rainy. If you wanted to get somewhere really fast, I guess you could just teleport yourself. But only very powerful witches could do that and Lilith hadn't ever spoken much about it to me — I'd just heard rumours that it could be done. Broomsticks were just for fun, and as I stood beside my own broomstick I realised I was about to fly!

Chapter 5

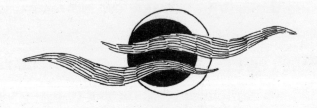

I soon found out that riding a broomstick isn't at all like riding a bike – unless your bike has a personality of its own.

'Every witchling needs to learn to ride a broomstick,' Lilith said. 'It's tradition, even if we don't ever really need one for transportation nowadays.'

'But they're lots of fun,' said Verity. She climbed onto her broomstick. 'Up, up and away!'

Her broomstick whizzed into the sky and my mouth fell open as I watched Verity fly up and up and through the sky, and then she started to fly upside down!

'Will I ever be able to do that?' I asked Lilith. I suddenly really wanted to be able to fly upside down. But would I ever be able to fly like Verity? Would I ever be good enough to be a Broomstick Rider? What if I fell off? It was an awfully long way to fall and would hurt a lot.

'Come on,' Verity shouted, whizzing past my ear. 'Get on your broomsticks, you two!'

'Only try it if you want to,' Lilith said to me.

I gritted my teeth and grasped my broomstick tight. It immediately flew out of my hands.

'Oh – oh no!' That wasn't supposed to happen. I thought we'd just take off gently and that it would be like riding on the magic carpet – but my broomstick was much more powerful than that. It was almost like the broomstick was alive.

Verity laughed and laughed while the broomstick hovered above me, looking like it wasn't quite sure what to do next.

'Something you did frightened it,' Lilith said. 'Call it to you.'

'Come,' I said. But the broomstick didn't come.

'She's just not a natural rider like me, Lilith,' Verity shouted. Verity was swinging from her broomstick like a trapeze artist now. I knew she was joking, but I couldn't help being irritated.

'Try again,' Lilith said.

'Come . . . Please.'

This time the broomstick drifted close enough for me to take hold of it.

'It's not that different to riding a bike,' Lilith said.

'Only it can fly really high,' I said quietly.

'Yes, and doesn't have pedals.'

I must have looked worried.

'You don't have to ride it yet if you don't want to,' Lilith told me again.

But I did want to.

I sat astride my broomstick as if it were a bike.

'Stay low and go slow,' I said to it.

'Next you'll be asking if you can have training twigs,' Verity said, as she swooped down to the ground and climbed off her broomstick.

I ignored her.

The broomstick did as I said and only flew a metre or so off the ground and glided along at a slow speed. It was a bit of a shaky, wobbly ride as

I kept trying to balance on the narrow stick.

'Come on, Lilith,' Verity called to her. 'Show us what you can do.'

Lilith climbed onto her broomstick and glided up into the air, as gently as a feather. She made it look so easy.

'It is rather fun, isn't it?' Lilith laughed. 'I'd forgotten how much fun it is!'

As she spoke an amazing thing happened. The twigs at the end of her broomstick started to change. They turned into lilies!

'Oh Lilith, your broomstick!' I cried. I almost fell off my broomstick when I let go with one hand so I could point at it.

Lilith looked behind her.

'It's blossomed,' shouted Verity. 'It must be pleased to be flown again!'

Was that the reason Verity's broomstick had roses and Lilith's one had lilies? I needed to fly mine more. I wanted my broomstick to look as beautiful as theirs did instead of the plain, ordinary-looking broomstick that I had.

I was just beginning to not feel so nervous when Lilith said that I had to land, and that the lesson was over. I was only allowed to fly my new broomstick for ten minutes the first time, twenty minutes the second – gradually increasing the amount I flew until I reached one hour. One hour was the maximum amount of time I'd be allowed to fly it for the time being. I couldn't believe it! How was I going to get as good as Verity and the Broomstick Riders if I was only allowed to fly for an hour at a time? It made me feel quite cross.

Lilith went on to explain that I needed to make sure I gave the broomstick a good rest in between flights, too.

'But why?' I asked Lilith as my feet touched the grass again. I didn't even think ten minutes had passed. It hadn't seemed very long at all.

Lilith explained that a new broomstick isn't used to flying or being ridden and needs to build up its strength slowly so it doesn't become overtired. 'It's like a puppy going for its first walk – even though it might seem like the puppy isn't tired and could go on, it's important not to overdo it.'

I looked at my ordinary broomstick. I'd really been excited, and even enjoyed flying and now I had to stop and wait. It all seemed so unfair.

I didn't have a choice but to do what Lilith said.

Gradually I built up the amount of time I flew and the broomstick became a little bit stronger each day. Within a few days, I was flying for an hour, and the more I flew the better at broomstick flying I became. I didn't wobble so much, and I was soon going as high up as the very tops of the houses on Coven Road.

While the broomstick was going slowly I learnt how to turn corners by leaning to the right or left – depending on which way I wanted to go. By Wednesday I even got brave enough to wave at Lilith before quickly putting my hand back on the broomstick handle. It was definitely safer to hold on with two hands than one.

Lilith always watched me and usually Pegatha came out into the garden too. Even Verity came along sometimes.

'Go higher!' she shouted, and I thought that maybe I was ready to risk it.

'Higher!' I said, and my broomstick shot up like a rocket into the clouds and I screamed in terror. Verity laughed and Pegatha ran and hid in the flowers.

'Not that high!' The broomstick swooped back down, racing fast towards the ground. The only problem was that I was upside down and I was going to hit the ground headfirst. 'STOP!'

The broomstick stopped immediately.

'Up – and then down gently,' I said, and it did.

By Thursday I'd got the hang of it, and I'd really started to love it. I could see that broomstick flying was just going to get better and better. While my broomstick had become stronger, it still hadn't blossomed with flowers.

I wanted to ask Lilith why my broomstick remained so plain even though I'd been riding it lots, but I didn't ask her because I thought I knew what the answer was: I wasn't a good enough broomstick flyer yet. I needed to practise even more!

'Don't overtire your broomstick,' Lilith warned me again at the end of the hour. She was very strict about it. 'It isn't used to being ridden yet. It was a branch of a tree just a little while ago. An hour at a time is quite enough for now.'

Reluctantly I climbed off the broomstick even though I didn't really want to. How was I supposed to learn tricks like the Broomstick Riders – or maybe one day *become* a Broomstick Rider – if I wasn't allowed to practise?

'Just ten more minutes?' I asked.

Lilith shook her head. 'Your broomstick's been ridden enough for today,' she said.

Meanie.

'I need to put that Agreement Spell on you –
then you'd let me fly it,' I said, joking.

Lilith laughed. 'You don't cast the Agreement
Spell on other people, you cast it on yourself and

then everyone agrees with you! It sounds great –
but it's not what you'd really
want.'

I laughed too. 'Oh yes
it is.' Every day would
be like my birthday. No
more doing what I didn't
want to do and only doing
what I wanted to do. I'd
ride my broomstick all day,
have my own grimoire and
have fun with my friends.
It'd be fantastic!

At bedtime I asked if I
could take my broomstick
upstairs with me.

'Of course,' Lilith said.
'It's yours to do what you
like with – and a witch's

broomstick should never be far from her side.'

I liked having it close by, but I still wished that my broomstick was colourful and had flowers growing on the twigs like Verity's and Lilith's. Why wouldn't it be as beautiful as I wanted it to be?

Chapter 6

Our class always writes stories on Friday mornings. I really like making stories up. It's one of the reasons Friday is my second favourite day of the week. Sometimes I make up stories about witches but I never write the truth about Coven

Road. No one would believe
me if I did.

I was going to use one of
the new pens Lilith had given
me for my birthday to write
that day's story. I'd already
decided what I was going to
write about — a witch's
broomstick that lost its power
and ended up being an
ordinary broomstick that was
used to sweep up the leaves
in the school playground,
until a witchling found it in a
shed and looked through lots
of different books for a spell
which made it work.
Eventually she came across a
a grimoire which gave her

the spell, and they flew off together on a magical flying adventure.

I took out my English book. I was all ready to start writing my story.

'This class's marks for the last maths test was so bad that I've decided to repeat the test,' Mrs Pearce said.

What?

'Right now.'

I couldn't believe it. Mrs Pearce wanted us to do maths instead of story writing – that just wasn't right! Maths was for Mondays, Tuesdays, Wednesdays and maybe Thursdays – but not Fridays.

Mrs Pearce handed out sheets of paper with lots of maths questions on them. I was so disappointed. I wrote what I thought of the test at the top of the paper and gave Mrs Pearce a hard, angry stare before starting, but she didn't seem to notice.

'If anyone needs scrap paper to work their answers out on, let me know,' she said.

I couldn't wait for it to be breaktime and for the nasty test to be over. Even though I'm not as bad at maths these days as I used to be it still wasn't right that mean Mrs Pearce had given us another test on it. Especially as we had done the test once already that week.

I looked at the clock on the wall, willing it to be breaktime. The second hand ticked round the dial very slowly. I wished it would hurry up. After what felt like a hundred hours, the lesson was finally over.

As soon as the bell rang, all of us raced out of the classroom door as fast as we could. I was one of the first to escape.

'Slowly – don't push,' Mrs Pearce told us. 'You'll have an accident.'

Only Sam stayed behind – he was helping to clean out the cages of the school mice.

'Let's play broomstick racing,' I said to Angela, Ellen and Rajni as soon as we were in the playground.

'We're a bit old for that. We are eleven!' said Angela.

'Oh.' That didn't matter to me. I would still have liked to play. 'What do you want to do?'

'Chat about stuff,' Angela suggested.

I sat down on the bench next to them and kicked at a pebble. My friends were so annoying. I wished they wanted to play a game instead of just chat. It wasn't like they were even chatting about something interesting. All they were talking about was what they'd seen on TV.

Then Angela mentioned *Dark Dreamer*. It's my very favourite programme. It's about a vampire who solves mysteries and lives between the ordinary world and the vampire one. I have a poster of the lead actor and the rest of the cast on my bedroom wall and I never miss an episode.

'I heard there's going to be a whole night of *Dark Dreamer* shows on TV soon. They're going to be showing every single episode and chat to the cast. It'll be brilliant,' she said.

I thought it would be brilliant too. It turned out that both Angela and I like the hero in the show a lot. It wasn't so bad just talking, but I would have liked it more if we had played broomsticks too – it would have been fun, and given me some more practice while I was outside Coven Road.

After school, I went home with Sam to the Woodland Wildlife Centre.

'Hello, Bella,' said Tracey. 'Come and see our baby fawns.'

The Woodland Wildlife Centre has all sorts of wild animals in it. Once it even had a lame badger. There's always some deer – although not usually baby ones. That was very rare. And often there's a fox or two, as well as lots of smaller animals and birds.

The two fawns had been born a few days before and they were so cute I wanted to stroke them but Trevor gently told me I couldn't.

'We don't want them to get used to people and get too tame,' he said. 'We want to be able to return them to the wild and be as shy and wary of people as wild deer usually are.'

'Let's work on my bug chart instead,' Sam suggested.

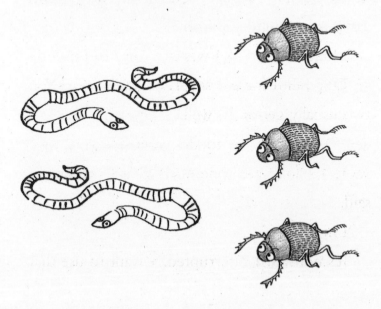

Sam had made a chart of all the insects he'd seen and where he'd spotted them at the Wildlife Centre. But I didn't want to — I don't really like creepy crawlies. I wanted to stroke the fawns. Why should I do what Sam wanted to do all the time? Why couldn't he do what I wanted to do instead? He can be so annoying.

'Did you have a good time with Sam?' Lilith asked me, when I got home.

'Not really,' I said. I was in a very bad mood.

'Oh.' Lilith looked surprised. 'Why not? You two usually get on so well.'

'Why do I have to do what everyone else wants to do but no one does what I want to?' I said.

'I'm sure —'

'It's not fair,' I interrupted. 'I want to use that

Agreement Spell so that everyone agrees with me and does what I want to do, instead of me always having to do what they want to do.'

'Tell me what happened,' Lilith said, patting the sofa beside her.

So I told her about Mrs Pearce giving us a maths test instead of letting us write stories like I wanted to do. And about Angela, Rajni and Ellen not playing when I wanted them to play and then not being able to pet the fawns at the Woodland Wildlife Centre.

But Lilith only smiled, which just made me more cross.

'Stop smiling,' I shouted, before she could say a word. 'It's not fair!' And I ran up the stairs to my bedroom.

Chapter 7

Fortunately the next day was a Saturday and I woke up in a really good mood, as I do every Saturday morning. The things that bothered me the day before didn't seem so bad when I was about to learn a new spell.

Lilith didn't mention the day before either, and got straight on with the lesson. She was teaching Verity and me a new spell to change the colours of flowers.

'*Zistoralda tamarala zistoral stoon,*' Verity chanted, pointing at a rose that turned blue. '*Zistoralda tamarala zistoral stoon.*' I was pointing at a daisy and the white petals and yellow middle turned into yellow petals with a white middle. Verity had brought her broomstick with her and when we had finished the lesson, we went out into the garden.

It was a beautiful, sunny day – perfect for broomstick flying. I felt a bit sorry for Lilith's broomstick propped up against the back door. She'd hardly been on it again and the lilies had all disappeared. I think Lilith thought broomstick flying was a bit childish.

Pegatha was sitting right next to my broomstick again. It had become one of her favourite places to sit.

'Maybe she's hoping she can go broomstick flying,' Verity said.

I didn't mind when our spell-casting lesson was over, like I usually did, because now we could do our broomstick flying.

This time, all my practice paid off and I was almost as good as Verity.

'Fly upside down like a bat,' Verity shouted.

I wasn't quite ready to do that yet, so I did some figures of eight instead.

'Very nice technique, Bella,' said Lilith, from the ground.

I wasn't ready to stop at the end of an hour – the time had flown by – but Lilith insisted as usual, reminding me to give the broomstick time to recover.

I wasn't happy about it at all but I cheered up a bit when Lilith told me we were going out for lunch and then shopping in the afternoon. We had to go to a load of boring shops I didn't want to go to, but we did end up going to see a movie too and it had my favourite actor from *Dark Dreamer* in it. I even forgot all about my broomstick as I stared at the screen and enjoyed the fantastic film.

I was fast asleep when Pegatha woke me from a deep, confusing dream by patting my face with her paw.

'Stop it, Pegatha,' I said, pushing her away. I opened my eyes. I hadn't closed my curtains and through the window I could see the full moon and stars as bright as diamonds. I climbed out of bed and went over to the window. The beautiful clear night was so magical, the sky seemed to crying out out to have a witchling and her broomstick flying through it.

I knew that Lilith wouldn't want me flying about by myself at night, but if I didn't ask her

then she couldn't say no like she always seems to. I looked over at Pegatha on the bed. She was looking at me with big round eyes.

Should I do it? Should I try flying on my broomstick alone for the first time? I thought that I should. And not just should – *must*!

I reached for the broomstick by my bed, and opened the window. Pegatha jumped off my duvet and raced over to me.

'No, Pegatha, you can't come,' I told her. Broomstick riding was much too dangerous for a little cat.

I was sure an experienced broomstick rider would have been able to take off from the windowsill but it was an awfully long way down if I fell. I decided not to risk it. It wasn't because I'm not brave – I am very brave. But I'm not stupid.

It would probably be a lot safer to start my

first night ride from the ground, I thought. I crept quietly down the stairs – I didn't want to wake Lilith – but all the way down I had the feeling that someone was following me . . . and someone was. Pegatha.

'No, Pegatha,' I hissed. 'Go back to bed.'

But she didn't. Pegatha raced past me before I could grab her. She can be very strong-willed sometimes. I went out into the back garden and climbed onto the broomstick. The night sky looked so inviting.

'Up, up and away!'

The broomstick flew up into the sky. Just as it was starting to take off, Pegatha raced out from the buddleia bush that Sam had given me, where she'd been hiding, and launched herself at the end of the broomstick.

'No, Pegatha – get off!' But it was too late. She was on the end, the broomstick was shooting

upwards and I was too busy clinging on to have time to shoo Pegatha away. We were too high for her to safely jump off anyway, so we both clung on to the broomstick as best we could. Pegatha's sharp claws helped her but I wished she'd stayed at home where it was nice and safe.

'Slower,' I told the broomstick. It whizzed through the air a little more gently. Night flying was brilliant, and although Coven Road was beautiful at night too, I wanted to see more.

My hair streamed out behind me as we flew out of Coven Road, past Angela's house, over the Woodland Wildlife Centre, and swished past the school.

'I can fly!' I yelled, as loudly as I could, even though there was no one besides Pegatha to hear me. 'Take me to the seaside!'

My broomstick obediently flew all the way to the shore and out over the waves and the fishes below us. Pegatha even tried to catch them as we flew low over the rippling waves. It was so much fun that I completely forgot everything Lilith had said about not tiring out the broomstick until I felt it begin to go a little slower. I wondered how much time had passed. Ten minutes? Or fifty? I was too excited to be tired and I thought that my broomstick should be too excited as well.

The broomstick flew a lot slower on the way home, but that just meant we flew through the pink and orange dawn sky. It was amazing. If it hadn't been for the fact that I knew Lilith would be calling me for breakfast soon, I could have flown on and on and on.

I put the broomstick by the back door next to Lilith's one and ran inside and up to my room. No one would ever know.

Chapter 8

'Did you have a good night's sleep?' Lilith asked me, as I yawned over my breakfast cereal.

'Mmm.'

Pegatha was curled up asleep next to her food bowl. She was too tired to even eat her breakfast.

'Pegatha seems very sleepy this morning as well,' Lilith commented, a puzzled look on her face.

'Mmm,' I said again. I didn't dare say anything else.

'What would you like to do today?' Lilith asked me as she sat down with her cup of tea.

There was really only one thing I wanted to do apart from sleep – ride my broomstick! – and I told her so.

'I can show you how to ride backwards if you like,' Lilith offered. It seemed like she was beginning to enjoy broomstick riding again.

I thought that would be a great idea. We went out through the back door and I picked up my broomstick, excited to be getting to fly again so soon.

'Up, up and away,' I commanded.

But the broomstick didn't move. Not even a

little. In fact, it didn't have any zing about it at all.

'Giddy up!' I said, a little crossly. Why wouldn't it do what I wanted it to? It was like it was just an ordinary broomstick for brushing up leaves with now. 'Please . . .' I said desperately. I so loved flying on it. I didn't want to stop.

The broomstick trembled and managed to rise a little above the ground but then fell back down again and lay still.

'How very strange,' said Lilith. 'Let me see.' She frowned as she picked up my broomstick and examined it carefully.

'What's wrong with it?' I asked.

'Perhaps it's too tired,' Lilith said. 'It shouldn't be though. Young broomsticks should be able to cope with one hour's flying a day.'

Fortunately she was looking at the broomstick so she didn't see my guilty face.

Lilith was very gentle as she handled the broomstick – she treated it almost as if it were a living thing and not just a piece of wood.

'I haven't used up all the magic, have I?' I asked her.

'No – that's not possible,' Lilith said. 'At least, I've never heard of it happening before.'

Oh no. What if I'd ridden it so much that I *had* used up all the magic? What if it never worked again?

She smoothed her hands over the broomstick and I was almost sure I heard it give a small sigh.

'It's exhausted,' said Lilith. 'You must have been over-riding it when I wasn't supervising you.'

I bit my bottom lip. At least she didn't know the whole truth.

Lilith looked cross. 'A witch's broomstick is not a machine. Just because it can't speak, it doesn't mean it doesn't have feelings or get tired.'

'But it's just wood!' I cried. 'How could it have feelings or get tired?'

Lilith shook her head. 'It is a living thing and as such needs to be treated with kindness and respect. Did you even ask it politely to fly for you?'

'Well . . .' I had said please when it had stopped flying but I hadn't really said anything nice before then. I thought it only understood words like 'up' and 'down' and 'right' and 'left' and 'giddy up' – and even that seemed clever for a broomstick.

'There'll be no flying for this broomstick for the rest of today,' Lilith said firmly, 'and maybe no flying it for the rest of the week. I'll tell you when it's ready to go again.'

No! I didn't want my broomstick to rest. I wanted to be outside flying about. The sky was blue with little puffy clouds. It was a perfect day for flying.

I also felt cross with the broomstick because it had made Lilith cross with me.

'I could cast a spell on your bedroom rug to turn it into a magic carpet and you could fly on that instead,' Lilith offered.

I told her I didn't want to. I didn't like it when Lilith told me off and I felt angry with her for doing so.

I left the broomstick lying on my bedroom floor when I went to bed but I felt like it was watching me and silently accusing me of cruelty to broomsticks so I put it at the back of my wardrobe in the dark and closed the door on it.

Monday was a terrible day. Mrs Pearce made me stay in at breaktime because I'd written, *This is a waste of time* on my maths test. Then the mashed potatoes had gone when it was my turn to be served at lunch and all that was left were some grey-looking boiled potatoes.

'Are you sure there isn't any more mash? Couldn't you just check?' I asked desperately, but the dinner lady said she was and she couldn't.

Then all Angela, Ellen and Rajni wanted to do was chat about boring stuff and all Sam wanted to do was clean out the mouse cage.

To make things worse, everything felt really difficult because I was still tired from being up all night on Saturday.

Things didn't get any better when I arrived back home from school.

The first thing I saw was my broomstick lying on the sofa beside Lilith. 'What's that doing there?'

'I found it at the back of your wardrobe when I was hanging up some of your clothes,' said Lilith.

'Oh,' I said.

'It was obviously very distressed,' she continued.

'How could a piece of wood be distressed?' I replied guiltily.

'It's very sensitive and needs sunlight. Only a little while ago it was happily living in the forest rather than your wardrobe, so I took it out into the garden with me when I was doing some gardening. The buddleia that Sam gave you is really taking root,' Lilith said.

But I was still feeling too cross with Mrs Pearce and the dinner lady and *everyone* to really listen to her so I went up to my room.

I was so fed up. Nothing seemed to be going right and everything felt annoying. Why couldn't things just go my way for a change?

It began as just a little thought, but then it grew and grew until it was all I could think about. The Agreement Spell in Lilith's grimoire . . .

I kept thinking about how good it would be to have everyone agree with me, to do the things I wanted to do and not tell me off or make me annoyed. I kept remembering that Lilith had said it was an easy spell and I'm very good at spell-casting.

When I was first adopted I used to worry all the time that if I did anything wrong, Lilith might not want to be my mum any more. Lilith had said that would never happen and she'd always *always* be my mum, but I didn't like the way she looked at me when she was cross. And that only happened when she didn't agree with me.

I looked over at my broomstick still lying on the sofa propped up with a cushion. I had flown alone and at night when I wasn't allowed to, and that had turned out all right. My confidence grew. If I could fly to the sea under the stars, then I was sure I could handle one little spell.

Officially, I'm not allowed to use a spell I haven't been properly taught even if I am inside Coven Road. If a witchling tried to cast a spell that they didn't really know and hadn't been taught properly and they cast it wrongly – well, anything might happen. That was the trouble with magic – it had to be done right, or else it tended to take on a life of its own.

But Lilith didn't often describe spells as very easy, like she had with this one. If she did, she would always add something like, 'Only you have to be careful in case . . .' or 'You just have to watch out . . .' and other don'ts and dos. She hadn't said anything like that about the Agreement Spell. I realised that meant it must be really, *really* easy.

Everyone says I have a rare talent for spell-casting too. Lilith had said most witchlings, and lots of witches, wouldn't have been able to cast the spell I had done to encase Rosina Rowan in amber. So, if I was really careful, and concentrated hard, I was sure I *could* cast a spell that I hadn't been properly taught. With my natural talent, it would be fine.

I remembered that witches aren't allowed to use magic outside of Coven Road, except in very special circumstances, although everyone uses it whenever they want to when they are inside Coven Road. But Lilith had said that you cast this spell on yourself – so I'd be casting the spell *in* Coven Road, even though it would be effective *outside* Coven Road too. So I wouldn't really be breaking that rule either.

I could really do it . . .

While Lilith was giving Bazeeta, Brimalkin, Mystica and Amelka their food, I went into

Lilith's bedroom. Her room is a soft white with patches of lilac in the alcoves. It has lots of wind chimes that make tinkling sounds at the windows.

Downstairs, I could hear Lilith chatting to Brimalkin. He's been off his food for the last few days. 'Now make sure you eat it all up . . .'

I opened the grimoire and the Agreement Spell appeared on the page before me.

Whoever you command
to Agree,
henceforth shall be
bound to thee.

'You want to grow big and strong, don't you?'
Lilith was telling Brimalkin downstairs.

I thought I could just hear him miaow in
reply. But I didn't know if he was agreeing or
disagreeing.

The spell might not even work for me and,
even if it did, it probably wouldn't last for long.

The words didn't look hard. It looked like a spell for beginners. A spell that a witchling would easily cast.

I took a deep breath.

'*Morashi kalli morashimar kasasama ra zar,*' I whispered.

Chapter 9

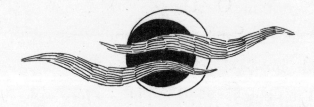

'Hello, Verity,' I heard Lilith say downstairs.

I shut the grimoire and raced back to my room. Pegatha wasn't very pleased to be woken from her sleep on my pillow. She gave a miaow of protest when I leapt onto the bed next to her.

'So-rry,' I told her.

A second later my bedroom door suddenly opened and I gasped in shock.

'What is the matter with you? You're as jumpy as a cat,' Verity said.

Pegatha hissed at her.

'N-nothing,' I said.

'Liar, liar, pants on fi-re,' said Verity, with a laugh, and I threw my pillow at her.

'I'm not a liar and I'm not as jumpy as a cat!'

Verity laughed and threw my pillow back at me. 'Are too!'

'Am not! Why won't you just agree with me?' I shouted, as I threw the pillow back at her, only just missing her as she ducked.

A funny look came over Verity's face. 'Fine, you're not a liar, and not as jumpy as a cat. I agree with you,' she said, and she flopped down on the bed beside me. Pegatha wasn't too pleased about her being there.

That was a bit odd. The grimoire's description of the spell came back to me.

Whoever you command
to Agree,
henceforth shall be
bound to thee.

Was that why she was agreeing with me? Verity didn't usually change her mind so quickly. It must be the spell! It must have worked! I didn't want to tell Verity though, because it was bound to wear off in a few minutes and she'd be furious with me if she knew she'd been enchanted – even if I hadn't really meant to do it to her.

The theme tune to *Dark Dreamer* started to play downstairs. I really wanted to watch it, but Verity doesn't like it. 'What do you want to watch that rubbish for?' she usually says scornfully.

But today would be different. We'd get to do what I wanted to do. 'Let's watch *Dark Dreamer*,' I said, holding my breath to see if she would still say no.

'OK,' said Verity.

Wow! We went downstairs together and sat on the sofa. I loved being able to watch my favourite programme without having to put up with Verity making sarcastic remarks throughout the show. I couldn't help feeling really pleased that the spell was working so well, and kept grinning to myself.

'Are you staying for dinner, Verity?' Lilith asked. 'It's vegetable stew.'

'Yes, please,' Verity said.

'I'd rather have fishfingers,' I said. 'They're much more yummy than vegetable stew.' Then I looked at Lilith and added, 'Don't you agree?'

The same funny look came over Lilith's face that had been on Verity's.

'Fishfingers it is, then,' Lilith said, smiling.

'Good.' I like fishfingers much better than vegetable stew. Lilith usually only lets me have fishfingers once a week and we'd already had them that week so it had to be the Agreement Spell working.

That evening was the night of the *Dark Dreamer* special – every episode that there had been so far, plus interviews with the stars. I so wanted to stay up and watch it. Lilith would never usually let me, but I really thought she could make an exception. This wasn't just any old TV programme – this was *Dark Dreamer*!

'Can I stay up and watch it?' I said. 'Will you agree?'

I thought I probably didn't have to use the 'agree' part of the spell on anyone twice, but Lilith *is* pretty strict about bedtimes. I couldn't risk her changing her mind before the end of the special, so I decided to say it again to make sure.

'Of course you can,' Lilith said. 'Shall I make some popcorn?'

We snuggled up on the sofa with the popcorn and watched the show late into the night. I smiled to myself again. So far the Agreement Spell had been a total success!

I wasn't sure the Agreement Spell would still be

working the next morning, and prepared myself for another difficult day at school.

When I got there, I started saying silly things I knew my friends would never normally agree with, just to see if they would now.

'Hedgehogs are rubbish, don't you agree?' I said to Sam. And that morning Sam agreed that hedgehogs were rubbish.

'And black is a much better colour than pink, don't you agree?' I said to Angela, and she agreed that it was.

Yes! The spell was still working. I was going to have a great day after all.

'Let's play broomstick racing,' I said, at breaktime. This time no one said it was babyish – Angela thought it was a great idea and so did Ellen and Rajni. We all had a great time racing round on our pretend broomsticks.

In the afternoon, we had a lesson about what job we'd like to have when we grew up.

'What about you, Bella?' Mrs Pearce asked me.

'I would like to be a witch, Miss,' I said. 'I think it would be the best job in the world – don't you agree?'

'Yes,' Mrs Pearce said. Everyone else's hand suddenly shot up. 'Yes, Angela?' Mrs Pearce said.

'I want to be a witch too,' said Angela.

'So do I, Miss,' said Ellen.

'Me too,' said Rajni.

I smiled at my friends. They'd never said that before. They must have really enjoyed playing broomsticks at breaktime!

'How about you, Sam – something to do with animals, no doubt?'

'No, not that,' Sam said.

'How about a Woodland Wildlife Centre owner?' said Mrs Pearce, with a smile. Sam

is always telling everyone
how wonderful the
Woodland Wildlife Centre
is.

'No, nothing to do with animals,' Sam said.

That was strange.

'What do you want to be then?' Mrs Pearce asked, her face as puzzled as mine.

'A witch like Bella,' said Sam proudly.

Oh no. Was this still the spell? I didn't mean the spell to do this. I didn't mean for Sam's personality to change, or anyone else's for that matter. I still wanted them to be themselves. I'd just wanted people to agree with me more and do the things that I wanted them to. The spell was going too far.

I tried not to worry. There was no way the spell could last longer than two days. Everything would be back to normal and I would laugh about it then.

The next morning my eyes were tired and they felt all scratchy. I'd asked to stay up late again and Lilith had agreed it was a good idea.

'Cereal for breakfast?' Lilith asked me.

Just as a joke, and because I was tired, I said, 'No, I'd like sweets for breakfast, lunch and dinner, please.'

'OK,' said Lilith, and she gave me a plate of fried-egg-shaped sweets. 'Enjoy.'

I stared down at the plate and then up at Lilith. There was no way that Lilith would normally have given me a plate of sweets for breakfast. My heart sank. The spell was still working.

'I don't want to go to school,' I told Lilith.

'OK,' Lilith said, cheerily.

I went back upstairs and crawled into bed, but I felt miserable. Lilith would never normally let me eat sweets all the time or stay up late and she certainly wouldn't let me have the day off school without a very good reason. Who was the person downstairs really? She didn't seem to be Lilith any more and I didn't know what to do.

The spell was STILL working when I woke up a few hours later.

'So you want sweets for lunch?' Lilith called up the stairs.

'No, I want proper food, please,' I called back. 'Can we have vegetable stew?'

Why hadn't the spell stopped working yet? I

didn't want it to work any more. Everything was too weird.

That afternoon I thought about asking Lilith if I could ride the broomstick – I was sure that would make me feel better, and of course she'd agreed to let me.

I looked at my broomstick. It seemed a bit pale. Perhaps it still needed to recover. It would probably agree to fly if I asked it, though, because of the spell. But perhaps that wouldn't be a good idea. I left it to rest instead.

When I got to school the next day I couldn't believe my eyes – everyone in my class was dressed as a witch!

'What happened?' I said. I had a nasty, twisting, scrunching feeling in my stomach. I knew what had happened. It was the Agreement

Spell. It was growing more powerful all the time.

'Happened?' Angela asked. 'Nothing – why?'
She sat down next to me.

'You're wearing black.'

'I like black. Black's my favourite colour,'
Angela said.

'But . . . I thought pink was your favourite colour.' It always had been for as long as I'd known her.

'Not any more.'

Our first lesson was science and Mrs Pearce asked us to tell her the difference between millipedes and centipedes.

'Um, is one bigger and one smaller?' said Ellen.

'They've both got lots of legs,' said Rajni.

'Can you tell us, Sam?' Mrs Pearce said.

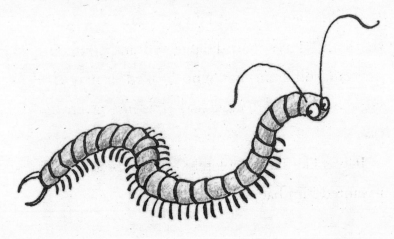

Sam was bound to know. He knows everything about wildlife.

'Millipedes have more legs than centipedes. But centipedes can move faster than millipedes. Plus centipedes can bite but millipedes don't bite. Do you want more differences?'

Mrs Pearce shook her head. 'I think leg difference and speed difference will do.'

I shuddered. 'I hate creepy crawlies,' I said.

Sam shuddered too. 'So do I – uuurgh!'

I looked over at Sam and my mouth fell open. I couldn't believe what I'd just heard. It was like the Sam I knew had disappeared and someone new and different, but who looked exactly the same as the Sam I used to know, had taken his place.

It was like I'd completely lost my best friend. I wanted him back really badly.

Chapter 10

The Agreement Spell had got out of hand. I hadn't meant for it to work this well. I hadn't even *really* meant for it to work at all, I realised as I walked home from school. It had just seemed like a good idea.

I'd had enough of everyone doing what I wanted them to. I just wanted them to go back to being themselves.

I wished I had never looked inside Lilith's grimoire. I wished I hadn't said the spell.

Then I realised what was happening. It was the grimoire! Lilith had said it had a power of its own. It had made my little spell far too powerful! I had to stop it. I knew what I had to do – I had to use the grimoire again, to try and reverse this spell. It had been so easy to cast, hopefully it would be just as easy to reverse.

While Lilith was gardening, I went upstairs and picked up her grimoire.

Before I opened it, I looked out of the window, thinking for a moment that I should maybe ask Lilith for help. She was kneeling

down in the garden, digging up weeds with a hand trowel. Pegatha was close to her, pawing at the soil as if she was trying to do some gardening too. I hoped she wasn't trying to catch worms. I didn't think they would taste nice.

It was such a lovely scene to watch. Lilith looked happy, and she would be so angry with me if I told her what I'd done. No, I had to do it on my own. All I had to do was cast the reversal spell for everything to be all right.

I opened the grimoire. I felt so relieved when the words *Reversal Spell* appeared. The spell was written in purple ink.

A spell to reverse all spells.
Only to be used with
extreme caution and in
the most dire of circumstances.

Well, this was certainly a dire circumstance! It did look more complicated than the Agreement Spell, but I had to try and cast it. I couldn't bear to have everyone agreeing with me for one moment more.

I decided to say it as fast as I could. *'Hazar-undba hestorial hanz. Hestorial hanz hazar-und.'*

And that's when I heard a deep, ominous rumble.

Chapter 11

The spell had worked – but I knew as soon as I'd cast it that I should never have done so. It was much, *much* too powerful.

I heard Lilith scream. I ran to the window to see what was happening. Our beautiful, magical garden was being destroyed! A tree by Lilith uprooted and crashed into the pond. Grass was withering, flowers were shrivelling up and bushes were vanishing.

What had I done? Oh, what had I done! I didn't mean for this to happen.

I tried to run downstairs but the door was jammed and when I pulled the handle, it came off in my hand. The chimney of our house fell past the window and then part of the thatched roof came away and frizzled to nothing. I was really, really scared. The magic of the cottage was being reversed too.

This was a disaster.

Worse than a disaster.

I grabbed the grimoire. 'Stop, please stop!'

But nothing happened.

I flicked through the pages. There had to be a reversal spell to reverse a reversal spell, but there wasn't time for a spell to appear. Suddenly I felt the floor shaking underneath my feet. A crack tore through the ceiling above me. Our house was tearing apart with me still in it! It could all collapse at any second.

I shouldn't have cast the reversal spell – it was too powerful! What if Lilith had got hurt by the falling chimney? I didn't want my mum to be hurt and I didn't want Pegatha to get hurt either. I'd spent so long looking for a perfect home and now I'd completely spoilt it. What on earth could I do?

'HELP!' I cried.

That's when something tapped on Lilith's bedroom door. Then the door swung open. There was my broomstick. It turned sideways, waiting for me to climb aboard, as if it was trying to help.

'Thank you!' I said, and I climbed on, still

clutching the grimoire, and the broomstick
zoomed up and out of the hole in the roof
where the chimney had been.

'What's happening?' Lilith cried when I
landed beside her.

'I'm sorry, I'm sorry!' I sobbed. 'I said the reversal spell in your grimoire.'

'Oh no!' Lilith cried, as she grabbed the grimoire from me. I could see by the look on her face how serious this was.

She frantically turned the pages of the grimoire. 'There might be time to stop it before it goes too far!'

Then bits from other people's houses and gardens in Coven Road came flying by us. The Reversal Spell was spreading! Redbeard's skull and crossbones flag flew past and ripped apart as the spider statue from Mr and Mrs Robson's house crashed on top of the buddleia bush and almost squashed Pegatha who was hiding there. Pegatha gave a howl and jumped into my arms for protection.

What had I done?

'Asiyarashar tisclamar torrevia saar!' Lilith screamed into the sky. She seemed to grow bigger. Her eyes turned red, her arms were raised high in the air and her hair flamed out around her. I'd never seen her look so powerful or so frightening. *'Asiyarashar tisclamar torrevia saar!'*

I hugged Pegatha to me. Please let Lilith have the power to stop what I'd done, I thought desperately. Please. I wished it with every wish I had, past, present and future, including my saved birthday wish.

Suddenly the wind dropped and the debris stopped flying. I sank to the ground with Pegatha still in my arms. It was over. It was carnage around us – our house was in ruins and the other houses in Coven Road had been badly

damaged too, but we were going to be all right.

But Lilith hadn't finished. She repeated the spell one more time and everything started to correct itself. The walls of our cottage went back up, the roof grew a new thatch, and our chimney rebuilt itself and began smoking gently like it always does. The Robsons' spider statue flew back to its place on their webbed roof next door, and Redbeard's flag restitched itself and hung from its pole once more.

Soon everything was back to the way it was before I'd said the Reversal Spell.

It had all only lasted minutes but it felt like hours and hours had passed. But how much had changed? If Lilith's spell had balanced out the Reversal

Spell, did that mean my Agreement Spell was still working?

I looked at Lilith. 'At least everything's all right now,' I said weakly. 'Don't you agree?'

'No,' said Lilith. 'I don't.'

For the first time ever I was relieved to hear her say that.

'I'm sorry,' I whispered. 'I'm so sorry.' And I was. Very, very sorry. I love our home, I love Coven Road and I love Lilith. But I felt sick. I'd let Lilith down. I'd let everyone down. I didn't deserve to be a witchling.

'What happened?' Lilith asked me.

I told her the whole sorry story about how I'd used a spell from her grimoire to make people agree with me. I even told her about the broomstick, and how I'd taken it for a ride and how it had given me the confidence to think I could do anything.

Lilith was really angry. 'You could have been terribly injured – killed even! Or you could have injured or killed someone else. Coven Road was almost destroyed, because you wanted your own way. You just wanted people to agree with you!'

I felt so ashamed. 'Yes.'

'Are you OK?' Verity asked, running over to us. 'I was so worried. What just happened? Was it a freak storm? It was so powerful.'

'Something like that,' Lilith said. She looked grim. 'It's over now, though.'

A few witches came out of their houses to find out what had happened. Lilith just told them that there had been a little problem but that everything was fine now. I knew I was very,

very lucky that Zorelda hadn't been home.

Then I remembered that my spell hadn't just affected Coven Road. I ran indoors and phoned Angela to make sure she wasn't enchanted any more.

'Are you okay?' Angela asked, when she answered the phone. 'You sound a bit sad.'

I was more than a bit sad. I was very sad and very ashamed. My voice cracked a little as I spoke to her and I had to squeeze my nails into the palm of my hand to stop myself from crying. Angela was my friend and she really cared about me. I liked her for who she was and I should never have wanted her to change.

'What do you think about the colour pink?' I asked her.

Angela laughed. 'What are you talking about? You sound like you've been drinking loopy juice.'

'Is pink your favourite
colour?' I asked again. I had
to hear what she would say.

'Of course it is,' she
laughed. 'You know it is.
Why do you even need
to ask?'

'No reason. It's great to hear you say that. Bye
then.'

'What? Wait – what's going on?'

I told her I'd been doing an experiment –
which I had been, sort of – and it was over now.
And I wouldn't be repeating it.

Then I phoned Sam just to make sure.

'Are you phoning up about the baby
hedgehogs?' Sam said. He sounded really
excited. 'They're called hoglets when they're
babies. There are four of them and we have to
feed them goat's milk every two hours – day and

night! If they were adults we'd need to give them beetles and worms. They like dog food too, but it has to be meat rather than fish variety. I've been so busy I haven't even had time to do my bug chart!'

I wasn't phoning about the baby hedgehogs but Sam had already told me that he was back to his usual wild-animal-creepy-crawlies-loving self.

'I was just phoning to see if you were OK,' I told him.

'Of course I'm OK. Why wouldn't I be? Weird girl. We're going to need to gradually wean them onto solid food and then Trevor says we can release them back into the wild when they're about four or five months old. It's so exciting.'

He was right. I was a weird girl. I must be weird to think that friends who always agreed with you were better than friends who were their real, true selves.

'You must come over and see the hedgehogs,' Sam said.

'I'd love to.' Anything that made Sam that excited had to be good. 'What's happening with the fawns?'

'Trevor's let them go back into the woodland already,' Sam told me. 'He's keeping an eye on them from the hide-out and said they were eating and seemed to be doing well and going back to their natural, wild ways.'

I was pleased. Trevor had been right not to let me stroke them after all. The fawns deserved to live their natural life, and be treated with respect. Which made me think of something else . . .

Chapter 12

As I put down the phone, I saw something out of the corner of my eye. My broomstick was propped up by the back door. For the first time I didn't see it as just a piece of wood but as something living. Maybe it wasn't alive in the same way that I was used to things being alive, but if it hadn't been for my broomstick then I wouldn't have been able to escape the crumbling cottage and give the grimoire to Lilith. If I hadn't done that then . . . I shuddered to think about what might have happened. I could have ended up destroying Coven Road.

'Thank you,' I said to the broomstick. It felt strange talking to it like that at first. But as I spoke I realised that if I watched and listened to it really carefully I could see that it was listening to me and I could tell if it was feeling happy or sad. 'Thank you for helping me. Everything could've gone terribly, horribly, really wrong if it wasn't for you. And . . . I'm sorry I rode you for so long before.'

I was sure the broomstick gave a small sigh.

'Friends?' I said.

Then the broomstick did something really

amazing. Hundreds of tiny colourful wild flowers started to blossom where just plain twigs had been moments before. Somehow, I just knew that my broomstick was agreeing with me and we could be good friends.

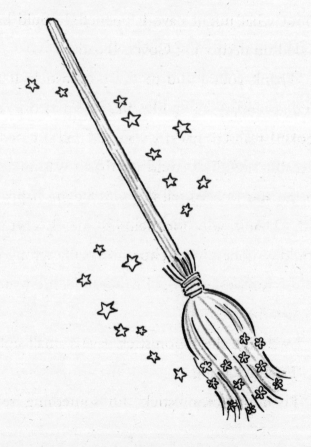

'Oh,' I said. 'How pretty!'

'I think you're forgiven,' Lilith said, seeing the flowers as she came over to us.

'But how do they do that?' I asked her. One moment it was twigs and the next moment flowers.

Lilith smiled. 'Witches' broomsticks aren't just ordinary besom brooms that have had a spell put on them to make them fly,' she said. 'Every flying broomstick is grown in the Witchwood. Thirteen rows of thirteen trees have grown there for as long as anyone can remember. None of the trees are ever cut down but every now and again, on the night of a full moon, one of the trees releases a branch and that branch becomes a witch's broomstick.'

'So my broomstick . . .'

'Is a branch from a tree from Witchwood, yes. Your broomstick was born to be magical.'

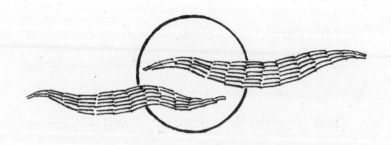

I took a deep breath. 'Will you forgive me too?'

Lilith hugged me to her in reply. 'Of course I will, but you do understand, don't you, that you must not use a grimoire until you are old enough, and never use magic without thinking it through first? A spell cast haphazardly or just for fun can be very dangerous. And if it does ever happen again —'

'It won't.'

'But if it does, or something else like it happens, as soon as you realise that you've made a mistake, whatever it is, and however foolish you might think it is, will you promise me that you'll tell me immediately?'

'I promise,' I said. 'I'm sorry that I must be such . . . such a . . .' I couldn't say any more words.

'Such a what?' asked Lilith.

'Disappointment,' I whispered, as a tear slipped down my face.

Lilith hugged me tighter. 'You're not a disappointment. You could never be that. Not a disappointment at all. You're very good at magic and sometimes you amaze me. A witchling of your experience shouldn't have been able to cast a spell that you hadn't been taught – even if it was an easy one.'

'Shouldn't I?'

'No. A witchling at your stage wouldn't normally have the power to do so, even if the spell had come from a grimoire. But that's why you have to be extra careful – because you are so powerful. It can be very tempting, as you found out, for witches to resort to magic when they have a problem – but it's important not to do so. Do you understand?'

I nodded.

'And what you think you want . . .'

'Everyone agreeing with me?'

Lilith nodded. '. . . can turn out to be something that you don't really want at all.'

It was true. 'I'm sorry.'

Lilith sighed. 'Everyone makes mistakes or does something wrong sometimes – and if you're a witch the consequences can be very serious. But everyone does it.'

'Even you?' I asked her.

I was sure Lilith couldn't have made any mistakes. But Lilith laughed and said she'd made *lots* of mistakes when she was a witchling.

'Tell me one,' I said.

'Well, when I was about your age my favourite

food was tomato soup. I loved it so much ...'

'Oh no.' I could see a disaster coming up.

'... that I decided it was all I wanted to eat.' Lilith shook her head at the memory.

'I should never have cast the spell.'

'What happened?'

'Every meal and every snack that was put in front of me turned into tomato soup as soon as I went to eat it. For a whole week, every food I tried to eat changed into tomato soup.'

'And what happened then?'

'Luckily the spell wore off. My mother refused to reverse it, though, because she said it would teach me a lesson. I still hate tomato soup now!'

I laughed, but at least her spell hadn't nearly destroyed Coven Road.

'And then there was the time when I was a very young witchling and I turned our cat  into a giant version of itself,' Lilith remembered. 'And once I tried to change the colour of the sky . . .'

I looked outside at the clear blue sky. I found it hard to imagine anyone would want to change that. It was perfect for flying in.

'Do you think . . .?' I started to say.

'Oh yes,' Lilith said, knowing what I was going to ask even before I asked it. 'I think your broomstick is ready to fly again now.'

My broomstick floated away from the wall and into my hands

as if it were agreeing that it was ready.

I thought I was going to be flying by myself but Pegatha jumped on at the last minute and we flew up into the sky and loop the looped and swished and swooped. And then Lilith joined us on her broomstick and I knew I was truly forgiven.

'I love flying!' I shouted to Lilith. 'And I love being a witchling too!'

Bella Donna

Coven Road

Most girls dream of being a princess, but
Bella Donna has always longed to be a
witch. The only thing she wants more is to
find a family to take her out of the
children's home where she lives.
But no one seems quite right,
until she meets Lilith.

With Lilith's help, will Bella Donna
be able to make both of her
secret wishes come true?

Bella Donna

Too Many Spells

Bella Donna appears to be a regular girl at a
regular school with her regular friends, but she
has a secret – she is really
a young witch!

She's working hard at learning her
spells, and is desperate to win the
Spell-Casting Contest. But when
strange things start happening at
school, Bella begins
to wonder if she can really
control her magic . . .

Bella Donna

Cat Magic

Bella Donna's favourite cat at home has always
been Pegatha, who loves to sleep on her bed and
follow Bella around like a little shadow.
But Pegatha begins to behave very strangely,
and soon Bella realises that someone has
cast a spell on Pegatha!
But why would anyone bewitch a cat?

Bella Donna

Join Bella Donna online!

Find out more about
Coven Road and Bella's friends,
and download games,
puzzles, activities,
and much more!

BellaDonnaOnline.co.uk